What to do today

Gwen Keegan

To Sarah & Nickolas
With love,
Aunt Gwen

Images by Dennis Keegan, Gwen Keegan, Keegan Carnahan, and Pexel.

This book is available from Amazon.com and other online stores.

ISBN: 1979740909
ISBN-13: 978-1979740906

I like popcorn
What a treat.
It's my favorite
Thing to eat.

The sounds it makes
While it's popping
Are happy sounds
Like it's hopping.

And it smells
So very good.
I'd eat it all
If I could.

Popcorn is so
Crispy and crunchy.
I eat it up
It is so munchy.

It's almost gone!
That was quick
Just a few kernels
Now to pick.

A few are left
That did not pop.
My tummy is full
I'd better stop!

ABOUT THE AUTHOR

Gwen McQuesten Keegan, retired nurse,
Now becomes a writer of verse.
I was very lucky
To grow up in Kentucky.

Now I live in California - with 'Grandpa D'.
Our grandkids call me 'Grandma G'
My pen I do employ
For children to enjoy.

We are happily retired
And I've become inspired
To write nursery rhymes and such
Which I enjoy – very much!

POPCORN

Don't you just love
The library?
There are so many
Books to see.

Books about this
And books about that.
Some are thin ones
And some really fat.

Books of all colors
Books about all things
I want to read them all
To see what each one brings.

I'll see what I can learn
From each and every book.
I can't wait to open them
And begin to take a look.

I like to see the pictures,
The stories that they tell.
I hope the ending is happy
Then I'll be happy as well!

THE LIBRARY

What's for dinner?
What's to eat?
I'm so hungry.
I smell meat.

I think it's meatloaf.
And I see carrots.
If we have broccoli
I will share it.

Mashed potatoes
Are so good.
Please pass the gravy
If you would.

There is cold milk
For me to drink.
Best dinner ever!
That's what I think.

What else do I see?
Oh my, oh my!
I do believe -
There's pie! There's pie!

DINNER

Why do we give presents
To each other on Christmas day?
What makes us shop and buy
And wrap up gifts that way?

Because God gave a precious gift
To every one of us.
God sent us baby Jesus
On that very first Christmas.

Jesus shows us how to live
In peace with one another.
How to be kind and helpful
And treat each one as brother.

So, at Christmas we give gifts
To pass along God's love.
We share with others what we have
Been blessed with from above.

Jesus' love, so precious, is
God's special gift to us.
That is why we also give
Presents at Christmas.

CHRISTMAS

We sit in the dark and quietly check
If what's in our stockings is what we expect.
We find oranges, nuts and candy
Just as we thought! This is just dandy.

We each also find one little box
I think it is too small to hold socks.
We quietly try to unwrap the paper,
Unstick the tape and pull off this caper.

I giggle when Sissy drops hers to the floor
"Quiet!" she says, and I just giggle more.
"You'll wake them up – we'll be caught!
Our early adventure will all be for naught!"

The tape finally unsticks, the paper comes off
I take off the lid and look in the box.
More paper inside! What can this be?
I unfold the paper, and what do I see?

It's a note from my Dad, saying "Go back to bed!"
"It's too early yet, don't get ahead!"
We wrap them back up. We've had quite a shock.
We sneak back to bed and lay watching the clock.

At six we get up and they're also awake.
We run in to begin our 'what small box?' fake.
We look in our stockings – the boxes are gone.
But Dad's smile says – I heard you at one!

CHRISTMAS STOCKING

Carefully and quietly we sneak
Out of our bedroom, to go take a peek.
We tiptoe out to the Christmas tree
Our stockings are by the fireplace, I see.

It is only one in the morning now
And Dad said we must sleep somehow.
All the way until five or six
Then we can unwrap our gifts.

When it is cold outside
The fireplace feels so warm.
I lay on the floor in front of it
In my jammies, safe from harm.

My sisters sit on the blanket with me
And the dog will join us too.
Sometimes I go to sleep right here
When the day is through.

I dream of all the fun we had
All throughout the day.
We went to the pumpkin patch
Then to the park to play.

We carved our pumpkins faces
And toasted all the seeds.
We sat by the fire to eat them.
They all disappeared with speed!

We had cocoa with marshmallows,
Those little ones that are yummy.
On the floor in front of the fireplace
We warm our face and tummy.

It is cold and windy outside
But in here we are nice and warm
Sitting by our fireplace
Safe from the outside storm.

FIREPLACE

We call out "You're getting warmer"
When one of us gets near.
Or, "You're getting colder"
Means you've strayed away, I fear.

If we get very close to one
It's called "You're getting hot!"
You don't want to hear "You're freezing cold!"
Are you close? You are not!

Once you find a fruit stick
You can eat it for a snack.
They are very yummy
That keeps us coming back.

When we hide one for Grandpa D
Grandma helps us choose
The best of hiding places.
(Sometimes it's in my shoes!)

One time we hid one under a pillow
And one time in a book.
One time we picked a really great place
Where no one thought to look.

I wonder if Grandma finds them
Hidden here and there
Days and days later?
Well, there's a treat to share!

FRUIT STICKS

We play "hide the fruit sticks"
When we go see Grandpa D.
First, he hides them for each of us.
Then we hide one for Grandma G.

One by one they come
Then they grow.
The next one to follow
Lines up in the row.

Babes became toddlers
Tots grew to kids.
Children then teens
Time flying on skids.

The high chair now empty
Just sits and awaits
The next generation
To come through the gates.

I look and remember
Each one of you
That sat in that chair
And in my heart, too.

Be sure that, although
You have outgrown this chair
You will never outgrow
Your place in my heart there.

THE HIGH CHAIR

This high chair has held
Precious and sweet
All of my grandchildren
Safe in its seat.

I like to help others
I like to be good.
I like to behave
In the way that I should.

It is such fun
To make someone smile,
To see them be happy
And grin all the while.

Kindness is always easier
Than meanness anyway.
If you're kind to others
Someday they'll repay.

The person you're nice to
And help out today
May be someone you need
Later along your way.

Do unto others
As you'd like to see
Them do unto you.
How happy you'll be!

BE KIND

What is the kindest
Thing to do?
That's what I want
To do for you.

Then I must say "Thank you"
Once the peas are passed.
This shows that I am happy
With the one who did as I asked.

Mama calls this 'manners'
And wants mine to be good.
'Good manners' means to always
Behave in the way you should.

I say "Please" and "Thank you"
And offer to help out
Whenever there is something
I can do anything about.

A helping hand to Grandma
When she needs groceries put away
Often earns me a cookie
If she has baked that day.

When Grandpa gives me something
I say, "Thank you" every time.
It makes him smile and hug me
Then up in his lap I climb.

I use my manners everyday
I like to do what's right.
It makes me feel so good
To be polite all day and night.

PLEASE AND THANK YOU

When I ask for something,
I always first say, "Please".
At the dinner table, I say,
"Please, may I have more peas?"

Mama says this is the way
To show respect for others.
She makes us all say "Please"
Even my big brothers.

One, two, three –
Let's learn to count.
Four, five, six –
That's the right amount.

Seven, eight, nine –
You are doing fine.
Ten, eleven, twelve –
You really shine!

Thirteen, fourteen, fifteen –
Now it's getting harder.
Sixteen, seventeen, eighteen –
You are getting smarter.

Nineteen, twenty, twenty-one –
This is so much fun!
That should be plenty.
And now the counting is done!

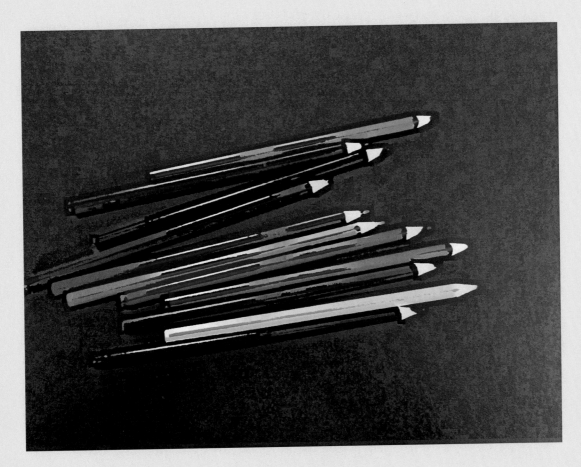

COUNT ON IT

Lovely little kitty, come and play with me.
Your fur is so soft. You fill me with glee!

You have such prickly whiskers and little paws - so cute.
Your purring is so musical and tickles me, to boot!

You have such pretty eyes and you look at me - so sweet.
You have cute little stockings upon your little feet.

Sit here in my lap. I could cuddle you all day!
We can take a nap right now and later we can play.

I'll roll your toy ball over and you bat it back to me.
Chase a ribbon with your paw as it flies up in the air -whee!

You curl up by the window with the sunshine on your back.
I think you are tired of playing now and want to take a nap.

The sun feels oh so good as I lay right here with you.
I hear you purring softly...and that's me! I'm purring too!

KITTY CAT

I made baby blankets for my grandchildren.
First there was one, then two.
First little girls got pink ones.
First little boys got blue.

The next grandbabies to come along
Got yellow, green or rose.
Some other colors were thrown in too
Whatever your parents chose.

Each grandchild is special.
You mean so much to me.
Snuggled in your blanket,
Oh, what a sight to see!

I chose soft and comfy yarn
To make your blanket warm.
With every stitch I thought of you
And keeping you from harm.

Each one of you are blessings,
Sent from God above.
This blanket that I wrap you in -
Each stich is filled with love.

BABY BLANKET

Easter eggs are oh so neat.
I just found one at my feet.
The Easter bunny put it there.
I'm going to look and find his lair.

He must have a giant stash
Of candy eggs and Easter grass.
I could fill my basket up with loot
And bring some for my brother, to boot.

I like jelly beans the best
I eat them first before the rest.
Chocolate eggs are yummy too.
I'll eat those before I'm through.

There are plastic eggs containing toys
For all the little girls and boys.
Once all are found, we sit and trade.
That's a very good deal I made.

I traded some eggs for jelly beans.
I especially like the greens.
Now we go to church today.
We fold our hands and quietly pray.

Eggs and candy are just for fun.
Jesus loves us, every one!
Our love for Jesus is the reason
That we celebrate the Easter season.

EASTER

Maybe sugar cookies too?
They are just the best.
They smell of vanilla
And sometimes of orange zest!

Mom lets me help her.
I must be careful, though.
I sit at the kitchen counter
And stir the cookie dough.

Mom turns on the oven.
It gets really hot!
I must not touch it
Not even in one spot.

The baking cookies smell so good.
Then out they come to cool.
Soon I'll get to taste one.
It almost makes me drool!

It takes a lot of work,
These cookies that we bake.
But it is worth the work because,
Our family loves the ones we make.

The cookie dough goes in to bake.
We take them out with the oven glove.
But more comes out than went inside,
You see, they are made with love.

BAKING COOKIES

Let's bake cookies!
Oh, what fun.
Lovely chocolate chip ones,
Can't wait until they're done!

Get into your jammies
And into bed you go.
Let's pick out a story.
I'll read it soft and low.

I tuck you into bed
We snuggle with the book.
I see you're getting sleepy.
You're giving me that look.

We read the book together
Then all at once it seems
Your sleepy little eyes
Say it's time for dreams.

Tonight, I read to you.
Someday you'll read to me.
As long as we're together
Then happy we will be.

Now it's time to go to sleep.
Today we've had such fun.
Tomorrow we will play again.
Good night my little one.

SLEEPY EYES

The sheets.
No treats
As it's too late.
But wait!
My toys are in
The water bin.
There's my duck
With any luck
He will float
Beside my boat.
I splashed around
And I found
My little fish.
How I wish
He was real
Then he'd feel
Slippery, squirmy
Like a wormy.
Mom says I'm done
That's enough fun.
She towels me dry
And I try
To stay up longer
But Mom is stronger.
Off to bed!
She says, instead.
Mom reads out loud.
I float on a cloud.
Off to sleep
Sound and deep.

BATH AND BED

All this day
I got to play.
Now it's night
I think I might
Take my bath
On the path
To bed and sleep
So I may keep
Myself all clean
To get between

"What's up with that?"
Said Johnny Matt.
"I don't know"
Said his friend Joe.

"It's news to me"
Said Debbie B.
"Ask Danny, though
He's bound to know."

But Danny did not.
Oh, what a spot.
What shall we do?
Nobody knew.

"Ask Linda Lu,
Or try to ask Sue"
Said Benjamin Jay
In his funny way.

"You go ask Terry
And I'll go ask Carry"
Said Sharon to Minnie
"And also ask Denny."

"Oh, nonsense!" he said
"Ask Wanda instead".
But the question fell flat.
What's up with that?

NONSENSE

Mom made it for me
The frosting is blue.
My favorite color
And it's chocolate, too!

Chocolate is the best.
I love the taste.
We'll eat it all up,
There won't be any waste.

My cousins will come over.
We can swim and play.
My older cousin dives head-first
Like I will learn some day.

My youngest cousin is only two.
We all watch out for her.
Mom tells us not to splash her face
Or crying may occur!

I get to blow out the candles
That sit on top of my cake.
And everyone sings Happy Birthday.
What a picture that will make.

What a great birthday!
There's cake on my face and nose.
I am happy and so tired,
And I'm sticky from head to toes.

MY BIRTHDAY

Today I am five!
Oh, what a treat.
My birthday cake
Can't be beat.

She makes yams just for me
And other things I must try.
Most times there is corn
And there's always pumpkin pie.

The house smells so good.
All the food looks so yummy.
Lots of family comes over
Then we all fill our tummy.

All around the table
We all take our place.
I am the youngest
I get to say Grace.

I am most thankful
For family and friends.
And all of the blessings
The Lord above sends.

We have food in plenty
But not all people do.
So, we share what we have
To help others get through.

Giving thanks for all we have
And helping those in need
Is what Thanksgiving's all about.
We are blessed, indeed!

THANKSGIVING

I love Thanksgiving
And all of the food.
Mom makes a turkey
And everything good.

Sometimes I have to get a shot,
But I don't mind – it's quick.
If I hold really still
I'll barely feel a little prick.

If they must give me medicine,
I will drink it all right down.
It is only there to help me,
So, I'll drink without a frown.

I only take the medicine
When Mommy tells me, though.
I never take it by myself.
That's not the way to go.

The doctors and the nurses
Are ever so nice to me.
They want to keep me healthy
And as well as I can be.

I like to come to see them.
They seem to like me too.
Sometimes I get a lollipop,
I always ask for blue!

We are all done now.
We'll wave to them, good-byes
And thanks for taking care of me.
You all are such good guys!

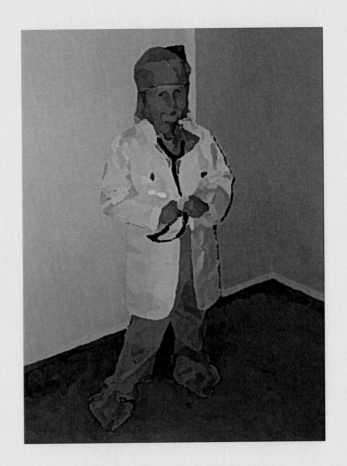

GOING TO THE DOCTOR

It is time to go to the doctor
To see how tall I am today.
They will also listen to my heart
And see how much I weigh.

They look into my ears and eyes
And feel my neck for lumps.
The Doctor looks into my throat
And checks my mouth for bumps.

"Jump over here
Froggy, my dear"
Said Lillypad.
In the sweetest voice she had.

"Let's play I Spy
With my little eye."
Froggy said "Okay."
And they began to play.

First Lilly spied something blue.
Froggy guessed it, too.
It was the sky
He got it, second try.

Then Froggy spied something green
To Lillypad, it was unseen.
She guessed seven times.
She even guessed limes.

But no guesses were right,
Nothing else green in sight.
"I give up, Froggy,
My head's getting groggy!

What else is green
What haven't I seen?"
Said Froggy "Oh, what could it be?
What else – it's me!"

HOPPITY FROG AND LILLYPAD

Hoppity the frog
Jumps up on his log.
"What shall I do today?"
Lillypad heard him say.

My baby sister is so sweet.
I love her tiny little feet!
And she has such tiny toes
It makes me want to tickle those!

Her hair is soft and fine.
Mama says it looks like mine.
She blinks her eyes and looks at me.
I'm her big sister, I'm almost three.

I will teach her how to play
What to do and what to say.
As she learns to talk
And as she learns to walk.

I will show her how to share,
How to dress and brush her hair.
We can play whatever we like.
I'll even let her ride my bike.

We can play together
Forever it will seem.
We will help each other
As we grow and talk and dream.

BABY SISTER

Or we could color in a book.
We could do puzzles, take a look!
Here are some "Dress up" clothes.
Do you want to play with those?

Here is my doll, we could comb her hair.
Or have a tea party for my Teddy bear.
Let's put my stuffed animals all in a row,
And tie up the lion's hair in a bow!

All my stuffed animals need to go to the Vet
To see if they need their booster shots yet.
Line them up in a row one by one
And we will get this healthy job done!

We could pretend to be teachers at school
And teach all the kids about the golden rule.
"Treat everyone else like you would like them to treat you",
This rule is so simple and always is true.

We could pretend that we are pilots, flying a plane
Up through the clouds, on through the rain.
Where shall we go on this trip through the sky?
We will have fun, where ever we fly.

Let's put down a blanket and sit on the floor.
Set out the tea pot and have a picnic once more.
I'm getting sleepy being down here, it seems.
It's nap time now my friend – have sweet dreams!

WHAT TO DO

What do you want to do today?
Would you like to go outside and play?
Or would you like to stay inside?
We will play hide and seek - you hide!

DEDICATION

To those who read to children – God bless you!